Just Be You

Published by
Crown Peak Publishing, LLC
P.O. Box 317
New Castle, Colorado 81647-0317
www.crownpeakpublishing.com

Library of Congress Control Number: 2007908585

ISBN-13: 978-0-9645663-5-4
ISBN-10: 0-9645663-5-4

First Printing
10 9 8 7 6 5 4 3 2 1

Published in the United States of America

Printed in China

With special thanks and much love to Honey, my Cocker Spaniel,
whose antics and joy for life fill the pages of this book.

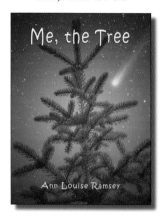

Just Be You

by Ann Louise Ramsey

CrownPeak
PUBLISHING

This is much harder than I ever thought...

all this learning to be who I know I am not.

As far back as I can remember, I recall...

I was busy not being me after all.

"Be like me!" I was told, even way back when.

I didn't really feel
like it was me.

So who I was not
became what I thought...

...had to be me, and I tried a whole lot...

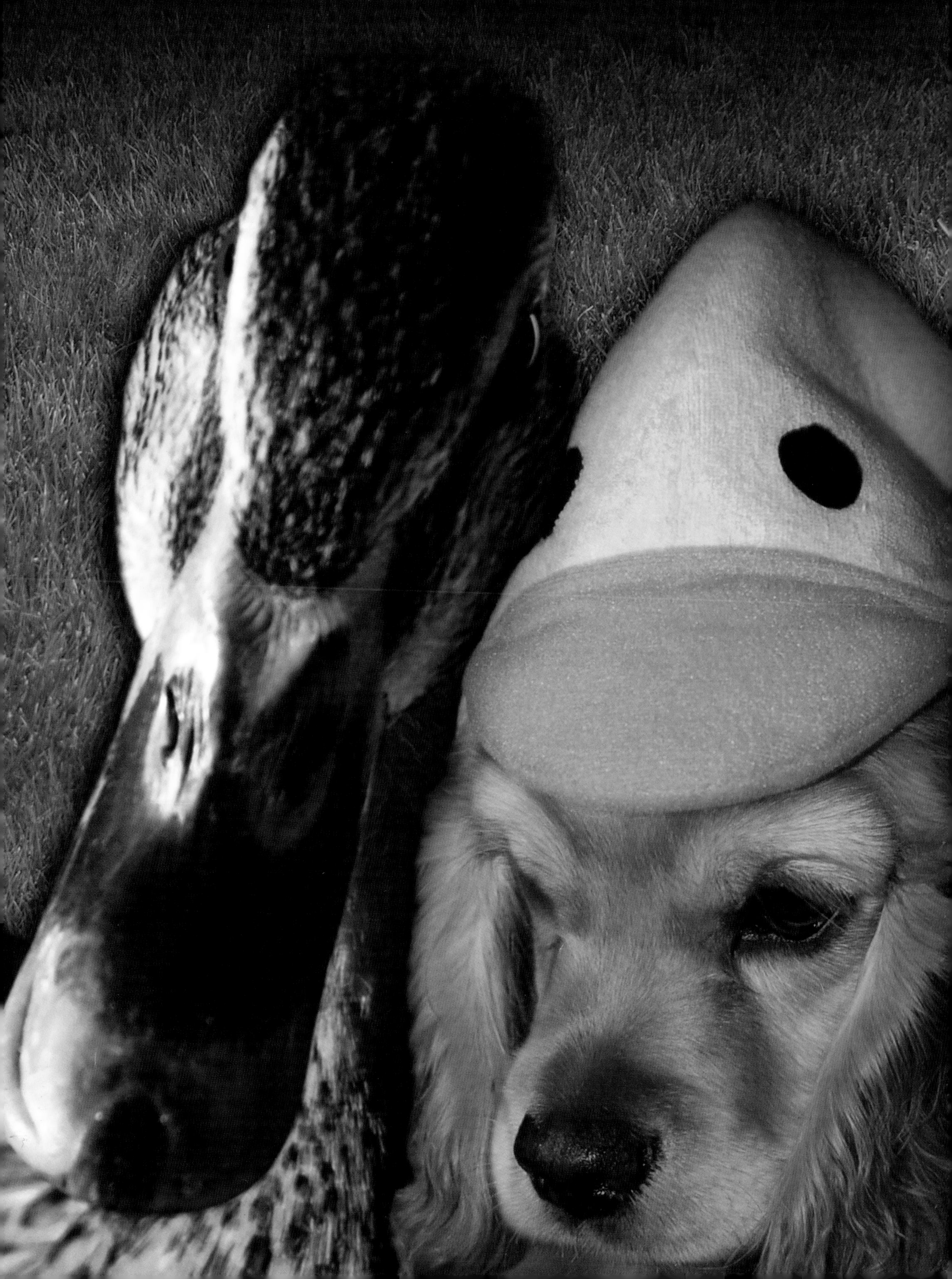

...to be like them, but I was just pretending,

and I kept my eyes open for a better ending.

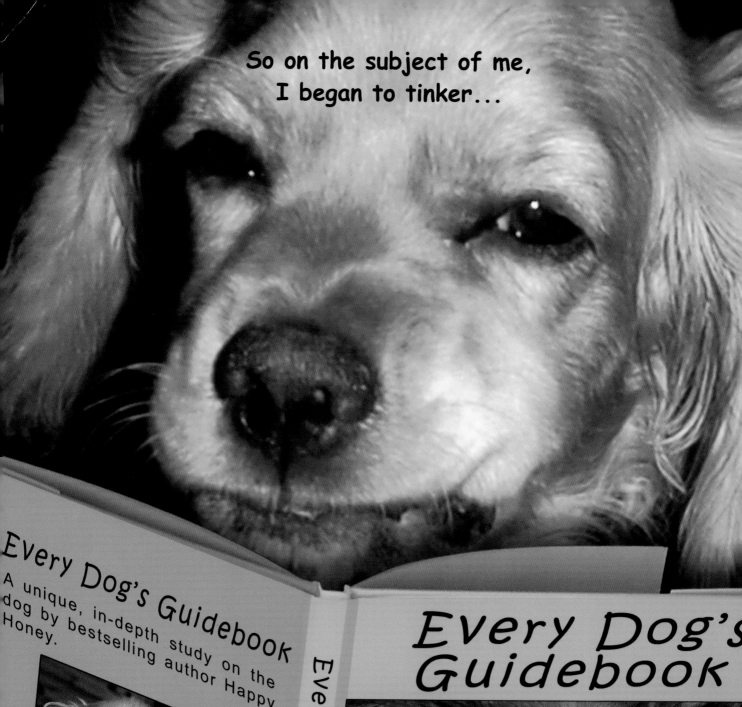

So on the subject of me,
I began to tinker...

Every Dog's Guidebook
A unique, in-depth study on the dog by bestselling author Happy Honey.

"Every Dog's Guidebook" sheds light on the true meaning of what it is to be a dog. Realize your true potential and have fun doing it! Whether you're a stay-at-home dog or a working dog, this book is for you.

Every Dog's Guidebook

Every Dog's
Guidebook

and on the reason for me,
I became a deep thinker.

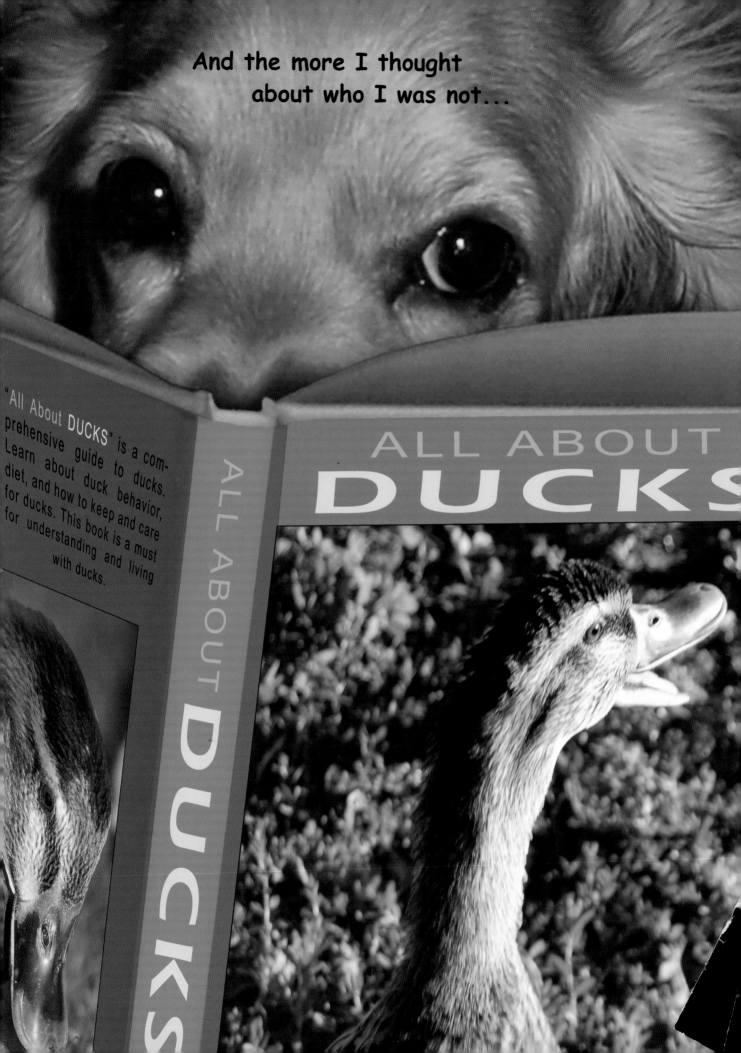

And the more I thought
about who I was not...

"All About DUCKS" is a com-
prehensive guide to ducks.
Learn about duck behavior,
diet, and how to keep and care
for ducks. This book is a must
for understanding and living
with ducks.

ALL ABOUT **DUCKS**

ALL ABOUT
DUCKS

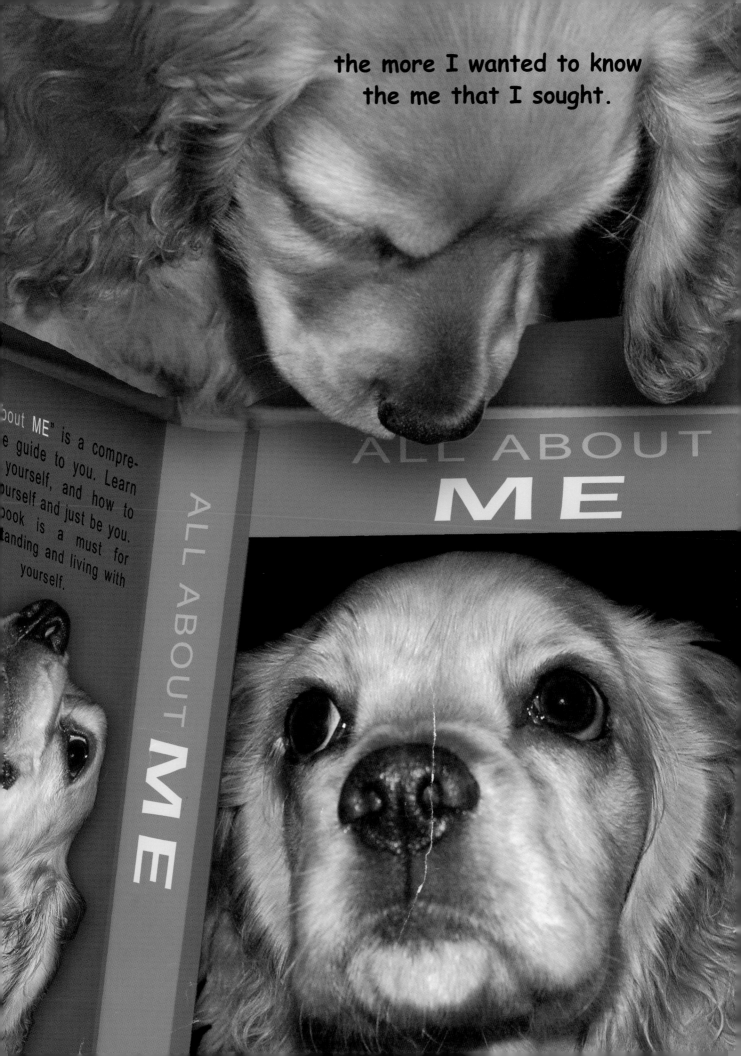

the more I wanted to know
the me that I sought.

"...out ME" is a compre-
...e guide to you. Learn
...yourself, and how to
...urself and just be you.
...book is a must for
...anding and living with
yourself.

ALL ABOUT ME

ALL ABOUT ME

ALL ABOUT ME

"Don't make things so difficult," said the mirror to me...

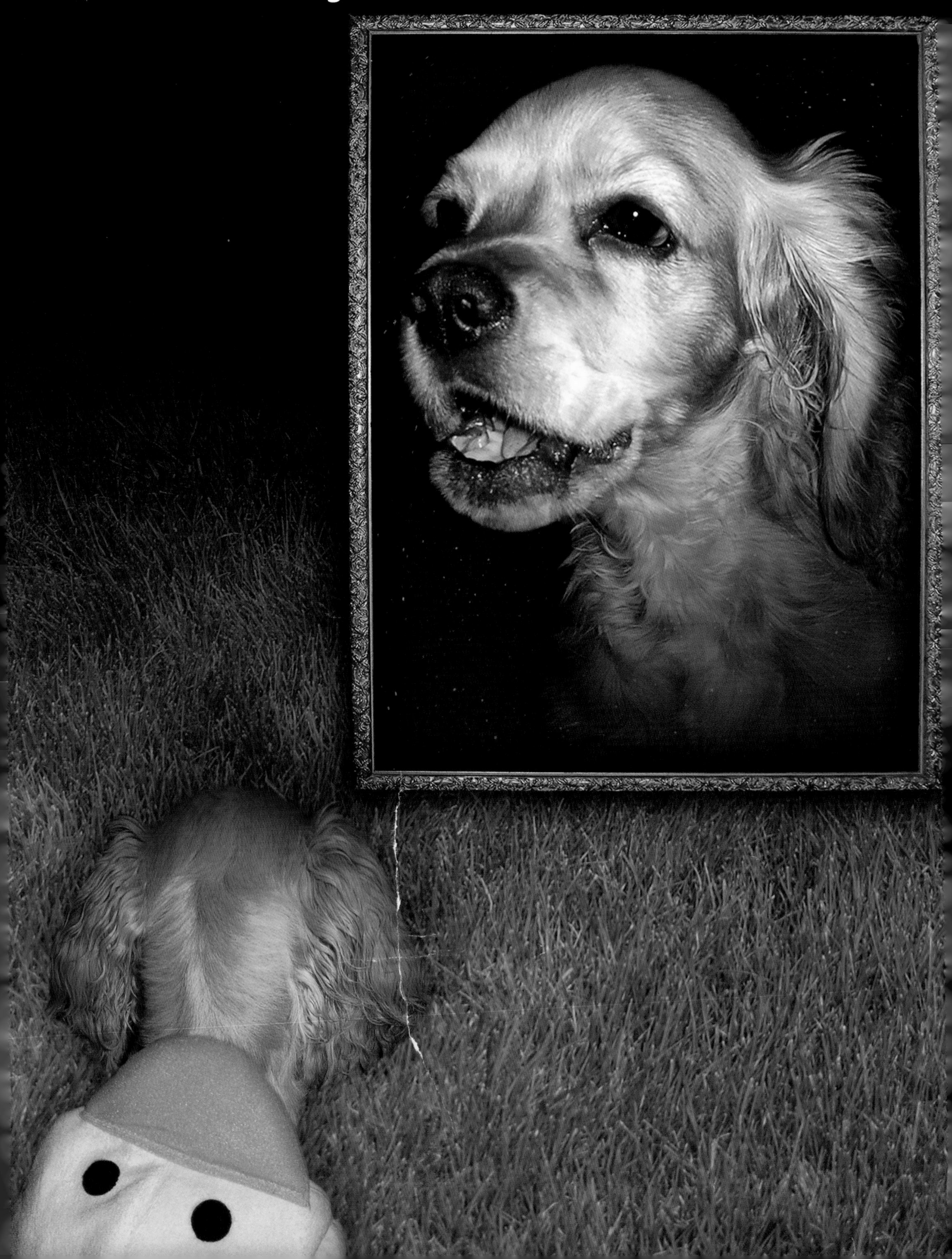

You are your self simply trying to be!

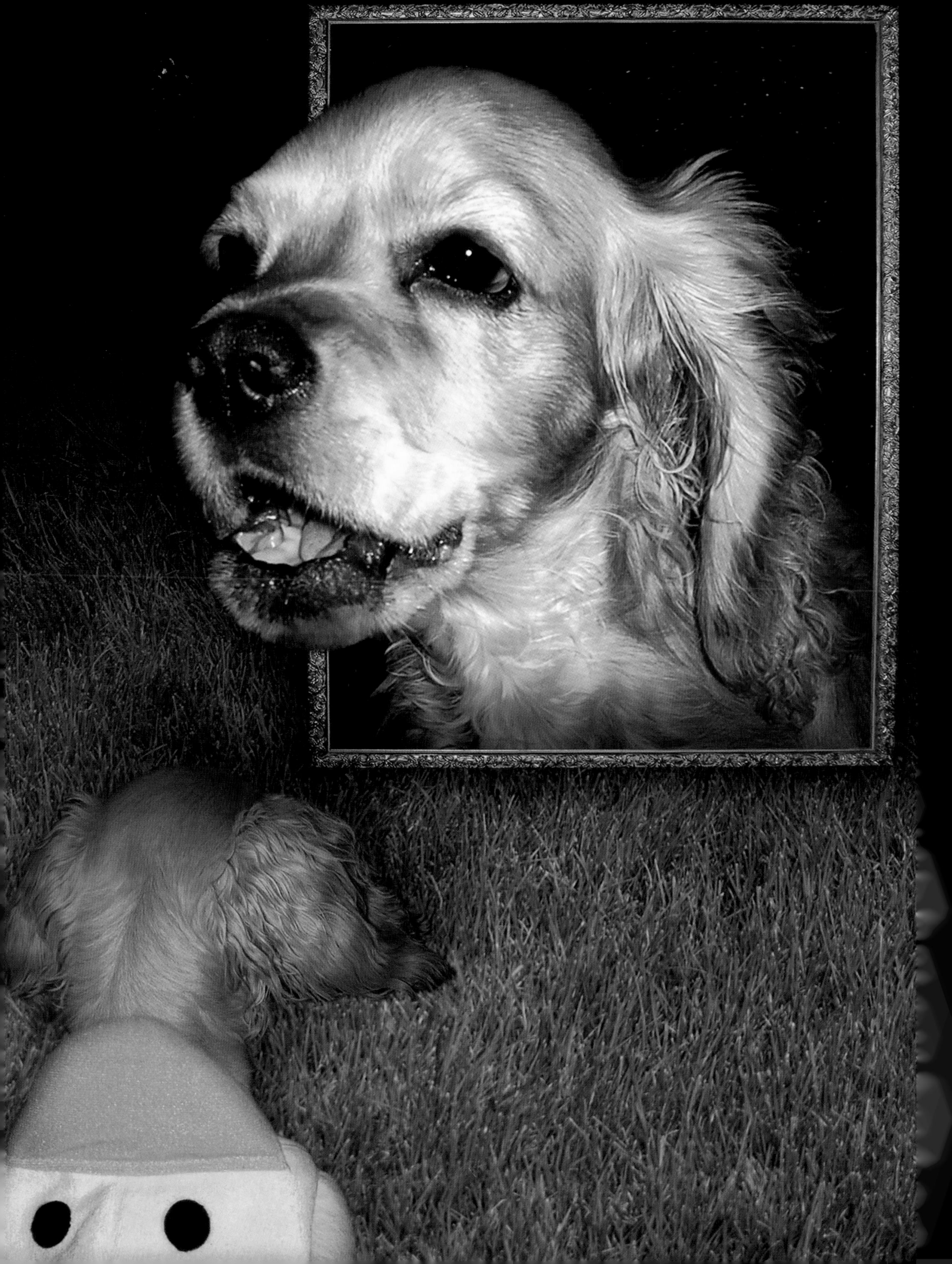

and I felt
who I was not
fade away.

what it's like to be me"... on and on, I rattled and

...suddenly I knew
it was not me that I fought,

So, who was I then? I was busy being them.

"Be like me!" I was told, even way back when.

busy being them kept you busy not being me.

So, who was I then? I was b... ...hem.

"Be like me!" I was told, even way back when.

"Be like me," the mirror said..."just be you!"

About the author

Ann Louise Ramsey, Colorado artist, photographer, musician, animal lover and poet, has been gaining recognition with her children's picture books, animal artistry and greeting cards, all of which can be found in book stores, libraries, gift shops and pet boutiques.

Skilled in computer graphics and design, Ramsey has found imaginative and delightful ways to bring her children's picture books to life. Winner of a 2007 EVVY Book Award (Colorado Independent Publisher's Association), her first book *Me, the Tree* has planted the seed of what promises to grow into a very tall tree for this innovative author/illustrator from Colorado.

Having performed music in a variety of venues for twenty years, Ramsey can now be found entertaining others with book readings and sharing her creative ideas on computer graphics, writing and publishing. Venues ranging from book stores, classrooms and libraries to special interest groups all serve as inspired settings for Ramsey to share her artistic vision and passion for creating picture books with children and adults alike.

Ann Louise Ramsey lives in Western Colorado with Honey, her Cocker Spaniel, where she devotes much of her time to writing, photography, computer graphics and artwork. In her free time she enjoys camping in the mountains and playing her fiddle with friends.

To learn more about the author, visit her website at
www.annlouiseramsey.com

Just Be You

Honey is a Cocker Spaniel who thinks she's a duck…because that's what she's been told by the "others"…who just happen to be ducks! But secretly, Honey asks *"Who can I tell that I am not what you see?"* and the mirror replies *"You can tell me!"* Share Honey's delightful journey of self-discovery in Ann Louise Ramsey's magical children's picture book *Just Be You.*

Bursting with joy and guaranteed to bring a smile to young and old alike, *Just Be You* reminds us of the importance of loving and honoring ourselves.

Magical realism comes to mind when reading Ramsey's book. Inspired by her love for Honey, her Cocker Spaniel, along with her talent as a photographer and imaginative work in Photoshop, Ramsey has created "magically real" images to complement her Dr. Seuss style story-poem resulting in an enchanting book. With captivating images to match this simple, yet profound message, *Just Be You* will find its way into many hearts for years to come.

Me, the Tree

Struggling to know its true self, one lone pine cone, in a forest of many, searches for an open meadow *"where no tree lived before"* in order to become the magnificent pine tree that lives within. Through *"patient believing"* this tiny pine cone fulfills its destiny as a tree and ultimately falls in love with all of life in Ann Louise Ramsey's children's picture book *Me, the Tree.* Follow the birth of a pine tree in this poetic parable about self-realization as this little pine cone with deep blue eyes embarks on a fanciful journey from seedling to adulthood.

Living in a remote area of the Rocky Mountains in Colorado for thirteen years, in combination with her love for her blue-eyed Australian Shepherd, provided the inspiration for Ramsey's book *Me, the Tree.* Photographs taken in the mountain forests become personified as Ramsey creatively incorporates her dog's blue eyes into every image, giving the pine cone a personality and an emotional attachment to the story as it grows into a tree.

This insightful tale of self-motivation and belief in oneself comes to life through enchanting images that capture nature's beauty and gentle simplicity. Inspiring and uplifting, *Me, the Tree* connects readers with life itself through validation of our own individuality and serves to remind us of the divinity that lives within us all.